CORDELIA'S PIG DAY

ELIZABETH BYRNE HILL

Elizabeth Byrne Hill.

ILLUSTRATED BY KATE ALDOUS

Pont

Contents

Cordelia's Family Tree
at the start of the story

King Rud Hud Hudibras
Cordelia's great-grandfather
'Hen-daid'

Princess Helen
Cordelia's grandmother
'Nain'

=

Prince Bladud
Cordelia's grandfather
'Taid'

Princess Rheinid
Cordelia's mother
'Mam'

=

Prince Lear
Cordelia's father
'Dada'

Goneril
Sister

Regan
Sister

Cordelia

 To All Readers

especially Beatrice and Eleanor

The story you are going to read is about a princess called Cordelia. She lived in Britain a very long time ago – during the Iron Age – at least 100 years BC. This was the time when people discovered that iron could be used to make tools and weapons.

Shakespeare wrote a play about Cordelia and her father, King Lear. Shakespeare didn't invent the story. He found it in an old history written by Geoffrey of Monmouth and it has been told by parents and grandparents to their children ever since.

Cordelia was already grown-up in Shakespeare's play so I thought you might like to read about her when she was your age. You will find out a bit about life in the Iron Age, too, and about the hill fort where Cordelia lived. Then you could go and look for the remains of an Iron Age hill fort yourself. There are hundreds of sites, especially in Wales, and it is sometimes a good climb to reach them. You may need a grown-up to help you get there but you can explore the site yourself.

Have fun!

E. B. H.

P.S. You might like to know how Cordelia says the special names she has for her parents and grandparents. 'Taid' (Grandfather) sounds very like 'tide' and 'Nain' (Grandmother) sounds very like 'nine'. 'Hen-daid' means Great-grandfather and rhymes with 'tide'.

Chapter One

In which Cordelia learns about the cleverest pigs in Caer

'Dada!' shouted Cordelia as she began to run the length of the Great Hill Fort for the second time. 'Dada, watch this.' And she leapfrogged a large boulder without really stopping.

Most people called her father Prince Lear because he was the grandson of the king. Cordelia usually called him Dada. She knew she was not supposed to yell, but before her father could say, 'Please don't shout, Cordelia,' she was too far away to hear. So Prince Lear went back to what he liked doing best which was looking at the stars.

And when Cordelia got back home there was no one watching her. She went to find her mother, who was busy making a pair of rabbit-fur slippers. 'Mam, Mam,' begged Cordelia, 'can I make a rabbit-fur hat? With ears!'

Her mother showed her how to cut the fur. 'Be careful,' she said, 'the flint is very sharp.'

Cordelia was concentrating so hard that she didn't even notice her grandmother coming in. When Cordelia had finished cutting out the hat, Nain said, 'That's very smart! I wonder if you would like to pay a visit to your grandfather and me for a few days? I know you won't be going very far, but you could try out your new hat.'

In fact her grandparents lived very near, at the other end of the Great Hill Fort but Cordelia was delighted. She jumped in the air three times and together they sang one of her grandmother's happy songs. It began like this:

'Three little pigs went out one day
To see what they could see.'

And then they tried making up some new words . . .

Cordelia loved staying with her grandparents. Her grandmother was especially good at telling stories and, as you will discover, Cordelia was very good at asking questions.

'Do you think you could tell me the story of the cleverest pigs in Caer?' she said almost as soon as she woke on the first morning of her visit. 'Please, Nain!' (Grandmother Helen was always 'Nain' to Cordelia just as Grandfather Bladud was always 'Taid'. These are the family names Welsh children still use for their grandparents, especially in the north.)

'Well,' said Nain, 'I will tell you the story, but first you must brush your hair and then we will have breakfast.'

Cordelia fetched her best bone comb and her new bristle brush and started to pull at all the tangles. Her hair was so long and the knots were so knotty that Nain had to help her. They brushed and they combed and they combed and they brushed until Cordelia's red hair shone like a bonfire at night. Then Nain plaited two long braids and when she had finished, Cordelia looked very smart indeed.

Just then there was a knock at the door and in came three boys carrying a pitcher of milk, a loaf of bread and a pot of honey.

'Please come and have breakfast with us,' said Nain very nicely to the boys, 'but first, would you mind taking some food to Cordelia's father, Prince Lear? He usually forgets to eat when he has been looking at the stars.'

Cordelia knew that her father had a very important job but she was also impatient. 'Oh dear,' she exclaimed, 'then the boys will miss the story!'

'Shall we wait for them to come back?' asked her grandmother.

Although Cordelia wasn't sure she could wait that long, she said yes anyway. She knew it wouldn't be very kind to start without them.

One of the boys asked, 'Why does your father keep looking at the stars?'

Cordelia couldn't quite remember what Prince Lear was supposed to be looking for but she did know that the stars look different every night.

Her grandmother explained, 'You see, sometimes there is a new star and sometimes an old star dies. Cordelia's father watches all night and when morning comes he thinks for a long time about what the new patterns mean.'

The boys nodded wisely and ran off.

When at last they came back, everybody sat together on the big couch covered in deer skins.

'Once upon a time,' began Nain, 'when Cordelia's grandfather, Prince Bladud, was very young, he travelled for three years and forgot to wash, or brush his hair the whole time. When he arrived home his mother said, "Go and fetch a bucket of water from the well and scrub yourself all over. Then you must brush your hair." He did as he was told. But it wasn't any good. He still looked terrible and his skin was all rough and sore. Even though he was a prince, nobody wanted to talk to him.'

'Poor Taid,' interrupted Cordelia. 'I would've talked to him.' She looked at Grandfather Bladud who was almost asleep in his big chair, and she felt very sorry for him.

'Well,' replied her grandmother, 'you weren't there. And neither was I!' and she put her finger to her lips so that Cordelia would be quiet.

'The young prince went away to think. He sat down near a place where some pigs were wallowing and squelching in chocolaty brown mud. When they had wallowed and squelched enough, they lay in the sun to dry. Then they began to itch. They grunted and grouched and they rubbed against trees, but it didn't help. Suddenly, with a loud squeal, their leader helter-skeltered to the bottom of the hill and all the others followed.

'As Prince Bladud hadn't got much to do, he wandered down towards the place where the pigs had disappeared. There he saw a bubbling, hot, yellow-smelling pool. The pigs had rushed in headlong and started to wallow and squelch again. Then they squelched and wallowed some more. When finally it was nearly their supper time, they came out of the water and looked about. They were so pink and clean that they hardly recognised one another. And they didn't itch any more.

'Prince Bladud was very excited when he saw this and he ran to the absolutely-magic pool, threw off his deerskin jerkin and his hunting boots and jumped in. Soon he was pink and clean and his hair shone like polished bronze.'

'Goodness,' said Cordelia, 'do I look all pink and clean when I've had a bath? I bet you hardly recognise me!'

The boys laughed. They had never had a bath and they wondered if it would be fun.

'Well, I usually recognise your pretty dress and your flippy, floppy shoes – and your hair shines like a bonfire at night,' said Nain with a big smile. 'Now if you listen carefully you'll hear what happened next. Without even putting on his clothes, Prince Bladud ran back to the fort and told everyone about the absolutely-magic pool. And they all said he looked very nice indeed.'

'Is that the end?' Cordelia couldn't help butting in.

'Not quite,' said Nain. 'Your great-grandfather Rud Hud

Hudibras was so happy to see his son looking clean, that he called the herald to make a loud noise on his nearly-magic cow horn. (It went brootbroothoothootho! about five times because it really was a very special kind of announcement.)'

'I wish I could try blowing the horn!' interrupted one of the boys.

'Shush!' exclaimed Cordelia. 'Go on, Nain.'

' "From this day forth Caer will be called Caer Badum," announced the herald. "It will remind us all that princes are much nicer when they have had a bath." '

(In case you don't know, Badum means Bath. It's like the Welsh word Baddon.)

'That is how Caer came to be called Caer Badum, Caer Faddon, or sometimes just Bath,' continued Nain. 'And after that, all the grown-ups of Caer started to have a bath at least once a year. And your great-grandfather, King Rud Hud Hudibras, decided that every month the Royal Family would have one bath-day each.'

Cordelia was delighted and started to clap her hands. 'What clever pigs!' she exclaimed. 'They found the absolutely-magic pool and they showed Taid how to get better. They must be the cleverest pigs in Caer!'

'Caer Badum,' muttered one of the boys. 'Bath!'

Chapter Two

In which Great-grandfather Rud Hud Hudibras celebrates a birthday

🏵 Chapter Two 🏵

Cordelia stayed with her grandparents for a whole week. On the third day Grandmother Helen said to her husband, 'My dear, isn't it your father's birthday tomorrow?'

'Yes,' said Grandfather Bladud, 'you are right. And it's a most important birthday too.' Then he turned to Cordelia and said, 'Do you know Great-grandfather Rud Hud Hudibras will be one hundred years old?'

'One hundred years. That is very old!' exclaimed Cordelia to no one in particular. She hoped her great-grandfather wasn't too old to have a party.

Next morning as soon as the sun began to peep over the horizon, King Rud Hud Hudibras called his herald. The herald made a tremendous noise with his nearly-magic cow horn and the walls echoed back. Everyone in the fort woke up at once. (If you want to imagine the noise that the herald made, try saying 'Phrooproopoop' nice and loud.)

Cordelia sat bolt upright in the fox-fur sleeping bag which lay beside her grandmother's bed. She listened to all the phrooproopooping and decided to put on her finest white dress in case it was time for the king's party.

Cordelia's grandparents were not very pleased to be woken so early and they grumbled a bit. 'Who told the herald to make all that noise? He should be arrested for disturbing the peace!' they said. But when they remembered it was the king's special birthday, they put on nice smiles and went to hear what all the noise was about.

The herald took a huge breath and shouted as loudly as he could, 'The King has something very important to say. Would everyone please come to the Grand Courtyard? Immediately!'

Cordelia's grandfather always wore his hunting boots in bed so he strode straight off to the Grand Courtyard. Nain put on her new, rabbit-fur slippers and followed as quickly as she could. Cordelia skipped along, holding her grandmother's hand.

By now King Rud Hud Hudibras was sitting on his special chair made from twisted willow-branches and resting on a great bearskin to make it look important. The herald made some snorty sort of noises on his nearly-magic cow horn and the walls echoed snorty noises back. (It sounded like Hrawhrshgeshgshg.)

Everyone was silent.

Then King Rud Hud Hudibras announced his plan. He told his listeners how very old he was (which they all knew), but before they could yawn, he said, 'I don't want to be king any more!'

Now this was most unusual. Cordelia's father had just
arrived and he stopped wondering about the stars and started
to listen. Cordelia tried very hard not to wriggle.

'Will Great-grandfather Rud Hud Hudibras still be my
great-grandfather if he isn't king any more?' she whispered.

Prince Lear put Cordelia on his shoulders to help her listen.

19

'I would like you to build me a tower with a room at the top,' continued the king. 'From now on, that's where I shall stay, and I shall have a splendid view without even getting out of bed.'

Immediately everyone started talking, and there was an enormous hubbub. Grandfather Bladud asked all the grown-ups to be quiet and to sit down and think. Since most of them were not very good at thinking, they just went on arguing. So Grandfather called out in a big voice that made Cordelia shake all over. It wasn't at all the voice of the Taid she knew. It sounded more like the voice of someone getting ready to be the new king: 'We will build a tower in the south-west corner of the fort, and it will have a staircase of one hundred steps to commemorate King Rud Hud Hudibras's great birthday!'

All the boys and girls who worked in the kitchen groaned because they realised how far they would have to carry the old king's breakfast. But nobody took much notice and Prince Bladud went straight out to choose the best oak tree to build the stairs.

A month later, when the tower was finished, the old king was carried all the way up to the top. 'I think I would like you all to go on calling me King,' he said thoughtfully as he sank down on his new couch. 'And, of course, Cordelia can still call me Great-grandfather.'

After that Cordelia's grandfather became the new king of Caer, because he was the eldest son of the old king, and her grandmother became queen. Most people started to say 'Yes, King Bladud!' or 'Certainly, Queen Helen!' but Cordelia went on calling them Taid and Nain.

'You will still be very important,' Nain explained to Cordelia as she tucked her up that night. 'You will be the granddaughter of the king and queen instead of being the great-granddaughter of King Rud Hud Hudibras.'

King Rud Hud Hudibras gave all the jobs and nearly all the rules to the new king. But he forgot to hand over the rules about bath-days. And bath-days were very important in Caer, as you already know.

When King Bladud and Queen Helen saw how happy the old king was in the great tower, they had a little chat. 'Cordelia, what do you think?' asked Queen Helen. 'We would like to build a tower in the south-east corner of the fort with a nice room at the top for ourselves.'

'The tower will have seventy-five steps,' added King Bladud, 'because we are both seventy-five years old.'

Cordelia, who was good at adding up, said it ought to have one hundred and fifty steps. All the boys and girls from the kitchens yelled 'no' very loudly, even though they were not supposed to be listening.

As soon as the tower in the south-east corner of the Great Fort was finished, King Bladud and Queen Helen climbed the seventy-five steps to their room and found they had a splendid view of the whole fort.

They were always pleased when their granddaughter came to visit them. And Cordelia loved visiting them too. She was rather glad there were only seventy-five steps.

Prince Lear, Cordelia's father, saw how nice it was at the top of the towers in the south-west and south-east corner of the Great Fort and he asked King Bladud, very politely, 'Could I possibly have a small tower in the north-east corner of the Great Fort so that I can watch the stars?'

King Bladud answered thoughtfully, 'Yes! But it will only have fifty steps. It will be made of elm wood because you are not yet a king. And anyway we are running out of the best oak trees.'

You might think that all this building would take a long time, but the carpenters worked hard. They knew they had a very important job to do.

In only seven days, they had completely finished the new tower, and Prince Lear climbed to the top to try and discover what he was looking for.

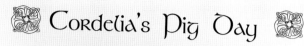
Chapter Three

In which Cordelia sees a sign in the sky

Chapter Three

Old King Rud Hud Hudibras was delighted when his son became king and he usually stayed in bed all day. But he came downstairs in his nightshirt about once a week so that people would remember he was still there.

King Bladud, the new king, was very happy too. He no longer had to ask his father for permission if he wanted to hunt deer and he could decide when there would be a feast. If he heard wolves howling at night, he said, 'Go and chase away the wolves,' and immediately a man with a bow and arrow climbed on the wall of the fort and sent an arrow into the forest to scare them away.

Every morning King Bladud was very busy. First he put on his long cloak and walked right round the fort. Sometimes Cordelia went with him. He said good morning to everyone he met and sometimes he asked the children if they had cleaned their teeth. When he saw children without any shoes, which was quite often, he said, 'Have you lost your shoes?' And if the answer was yes, he made sure that the father of the little boy or girl got some leather after the next feast. Then he went to archery practice for at least an hour because kings have to set a good example.

Every afternoon King Bladud had a little sleep and when he woke up he was delighted if Cordelia was waiting for him. Sometimes they drew squares on the ground and tried to throw a stone into each square. Other times, Cordelia showed him what she could do with a skipping rope. King Bladud didn't really think he would like skipping himself but he did like holding one end of the rope. If Cordelia was very lucky, her grandfather took her riding while he inspected the fields of barley and spelt, or visited the cows and the pigs.

King Bladud worked very hard. And when he came indoors in the evenings, he sat beside the fire with Queen Helen and she listened to all the problems of Caer. Sometimes Cordelia listened too and sometimes she asked questions. 'How do you know when a cow is going to have twin calves, Taid?' or 'How do all the grannies know so many stories, Nain?'

After a year and a day of working so hard, King Bladud began to feel very tired and he decided that he would rather not be king. 'Helen, my dear,' he said to his wife, 'I am getting too old for all this malarkey and I don't want to be king any more.'

Queen Helen agreed. 'It is rather tiring having to make sure that all the watchmen and watchwomen are really watching, and all the washerwomen and washermen are really washing, and all the children are playing sensible games,' she said. 'And Prince Lear is quite old enough to be king.'

So they called the herald to make another loud noise

on his nearly-magic cow horn to summon everyone to the Grand Courtyard.

It was the middle of the afternoon and, even though everyone was wide awake, the herald made a loud hooty sort of noise on his nearly-magic cow horn and the walls echoed back, 'Hootyfrootootyfrightyhightytightytoot.' (Can you do that one?)

King Bladud sat down on the chair of twisted willow-branches resting on its great bearskin, and began: 'I have been king for a year and a day. Now I think it's time for my son to do the work.'

Prince Lear was nowhere to be seen. Cordelia ran as fast as she could, up the fifty steps to her father's room.

'Dada,' she exclaimed when she saw him sitting with his head in his hands. 'Did you hear the herald? We all have to be in the Grand Courtyard. Now! I think Grandfather Bladud is asking you to be the new king.'

'Oh bother,' said Prince Lear and he tramped down the fifty steps to the Grand Courtyard, mumbling into his big black beard as he went.

King Bladud repeated, rather loudly this time, 'I have been king for a year and a day. Now I think it's time for my son to do the work.'

'That's you,' whispered Cordelia's mother and she gave her husband a little pinch in case he wasn't really listening.

Cordelia didn't think he had time to be king because he

was so busy looking at the stars. Her mother thought it was an excellent idea. 'Now he won't spend so much time in his tower and we will all have breakfast together every day,' she said.

Prince Lear sat down and started to think very carefully. 'My father wants me to be the ruler of Caer,' he thought to himself. 'Shall I say yes or no?' Then, very slowly, he stood up and said, 'Please, Father, could you wait till after the next new moon? I shall watch the stars very carefully. The patterns they make in the sky are signs and if I work very hard I can understand them. Each evening a very bright star called Hesperos arrives first. It will be my guide and I will learn if I should be king or not. Then I will be able to give you the answer.'

Cordelia looked at her father. Then she looked at her grandfather. King Bladud was looking rather surprised.

Suddenly there was a murmuring. The old King Rud Hud Hudibras was standing at the foot of his tower. He was wearing the tunic he always wore in bed and he hadn't brushed his hair because he had come down in such a hurry. 'Ha, ha-ha, ho-ho-ho! Clever boy,' he cried.

Of course the walls echoed: 'Ha-ha, ho-ho!'

'Clever boy!' the old king roared again. 'What an excellent idea!'

Cordelia couldn't help giggling. She had never heard anyone call her father 'boy' before.

'Shall we ask one person from each family to take a turn watching the stars with him?' said King Rud Hud Hudibras. 'Every night until the new moon?'

This was most exciting. Prince Lear had never shown anyone how he measured the way the stars move. Not even Cordelia. There was a long silence and Prince Lear looked at all the people who were waiting for an answer. There were only twenty-five days left till the new moon. Cordelia wondered if every family would get a turn.

At last Prince Lear spoke: 'Who would like to be first?' he said.

Almost everyone put their hands on their heads because that was the way to say *me, I would!* But Cordelia just stood there. She did not put her hands on her head. 'If it is supposed to be one person from each family then I can't be chosen,' she thought. 'My father will be up in the tower so I can't go.'

Prince Lear started to choose the watchers. He wanted to be fair so he picked one person from each family until there were six fathers and six mothers and six boys and six girls. They couldn't wait to start.

'What about the twenty-fifth night?' asked someone in the crowd.

'That will be for me,' said old King Rud Hud Hudibras very quickly.

Cordelia wasn't sure that it was quite fair because her great-grandfather was the same family as her father. And she was very sad that she had not put her hands on her head. 'Perhaps when I am a hundred years old, I will be allowed to do things like that,' she thought.

The nights went by and after twenty-four nights Prince Lear had still seen no sign. On the evening before the new moon was due everyone started to look out of their doors. They peered at the sky. No one could see a special sign.

'Tonight Great-grandfather will come with me,' said Prince Lear to Cordelia and her mother as he got ready to climb his tower.

But old King Rud Hud Hudibras did not come down that evening. He sent a boy with a message instead. The boy said, 'King Rud Hud Hudibras says he is very tired. Please would Cordelia be kind enough to go in his place!'

Cordelia couldn't believe her ears. The last night! There would have to be a sign. She gave her father a big hug and ran up the stairs behind him.

Prince Lear explained about the stars that look like a plough in the sky and then he showed her the Great Huntsman. 'The huntsman's called Orion,' he said. 'Nain's father taught her astronomy when she was a little girl in Greece. And when I was about as big as you, she started to teach me everything she knew. She used to take me to the top of the highest hill, long before they built the towers, and I learnt to repeat all the names. There's Tauros, the bull. We can just see him there in the west. And there's Leon, the lion.

But he's a bit slow coming tonight. There is even a princess called Andromeda if you look very hard.'

Prince Lear pointed to each one and Cordelia tucked them carefully into her memory. Then she thought for a moment. She remembered that her father had spoken about the very first star that peeps and twinkles in the evening. The one she usually called the Evening Star though she knew that it had another name.

'It begins with H,' Prince Lear said helpfully.

'Hester? Hostero? Hooperup?'

'No, no, no!' laughed her father. 'Nearly. It's Hesperos. It's a Greek name. He comes at dusk, as soon as the sun has gone. In the morning, his mother Eos comes to tell him it is time to go back to bed.'

'Does he sleep all day?' asked Cordelia.

Prince Lear scratched his head. 'I don't know,' he said. 'Maybe he just hides!'

They both laughed.

'Did Nain tell you that?' Cordelia asked. She loved hearing about the stars and she loved listening to stories about her grandmother. She knew that Nain's name, Helen, was from Greece because no one else in Caer was called Helen.

Suddenly Prince Lear said, 'Look! There is a new star.' Cordelia looked and there was a bright new star.

'Now, at last, I know what I have been looking for,' said

Prince Lear, almost to himself. 'The sign must mean that I have to say yes.'

When morning came, Prince Lear and Cordelia went down the Stair of the Fifty Steps and up the Stair of the Seventy-five Steps to tell the king and queen what they had seen.

'I have decided to say yes,' said Prince Lear.

King Bladud was very pleased indeed and he called the herald with the nearly-magic cow horn to make an announcement.

And that is how Prince Lear came to be king and his wife came to be queen.

Cordelia thought to herself as she lay in bed that night: 'First Great-grandfather was king, then Taid was king and now Dada is going to be king!' and she ticked them off on her fingers. 'So now I'm not the great-granddaughter of the king. I'm not even the granddaughter of the king. I'm the *daughter* of the new king.'

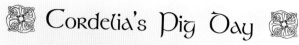
Chapter Four

In which Cordelia celebrates the first
Pig Day

Chapter Four

One day, not long after her father became king, Cordelia talked so much that her mother said, 'Please, Cordelia, could you just be quiet while I think!'

Cordelia said it was boring because you couldn't hear thinking. 'Mam, can I have a pig for my birthday?' she asked.

'But it's not your birthday,' replied her mother, without even pausing as she tidied up the breakfast things.

Cordelia thought for a long time. Then she said, 'Can I have a pig for *your* birthday?'

'Well,' said Mam, 'if I give you a pig on my birthday, then you'll have to give me a present on your birthday.'

'Good,' said Cordelia. 'I'll give you a pig.'

'Oh, all right,' said her mother, 'but it's not my birthday either.'

Cordelia thought for another long time. When it was bedtime she dreamed about the famous, clever pigs that discovered the nearly-magic healing water at Caer.

In the morning Cordelia woke up very early. It was the first day of *Saille*, the fifth month of the year. She often practised saying the names of the months: *Beth, Luis, Nion, Fearn, Saille*. She thought they sounded like good friends.

She had a feeling that this was a very unusual kind of day. 'Is it my birthday?' she mused to herself as she stretched and yawned. 'I know what,' she said out loud as she jumped out of her fox-fur bag, 'It must be my bath-day!' She put on her warm furry socks and crept round to see if her mother was awake.

The queen was busy shooing a magpie that had tried to steal her most precious ring, but she stopped shooing as soon as she saw Cordelia. 'Cordelia, today is the first day of *Saille*,' she said, 'and you know you always have a bath on the first day of every month.'

The sun was shining, the birds were singing and Cordelia was pleased that it was her bath-day. But something was missing. 'Can I have a pig for my bath-day?' asked Cordelia.

'Whatever for?' said her mother.

'Well,' replied Cordelia, 'then I'd have a special friend, wouldn't I?'

Now the queen was stumped for an answer, so she said, 'Go and ask your father.'

King Lear had been watching the stars all night and was still at the top of his tower. Cordelia climbed the Stair of the Fifty Steps, all the way up to the place where King Lear was looking at the stars. She was just going to bang loudly on his door when she remembered she had forgotten what her question was. So she ran all the way downstairs and when she got to the very bottom step, she suddenly remembered what she had forgotten. She began to climb again.

This time she repeated, 'Can I have a pig for my bath-day?' on every step so she would not forget. When she got to the twenty-fifth step, she stood still and did some more thinking. She thought very hard. And then she decided it would be a good idea to say, '*Please*, may I have a pig for my bath-day?' (Grown-ups are usually much happier if you say please.)

Then she climbed twenty-five more steps till she was right outside King Lear's door. Again. But before she could bang on the door, it opened all by itself. There was King Lear wearing his special robe for looking at the stars. You could not see his mouth when he was thinking because he had a big black beard. Now, his beard opened in the middle and he said in a big voice, 'Cordelia, today is the first day of *Saille*. I think it is your bath-day!'

Cordelia was so surprised, she burbled, 'Can I have a bath-day for my pig?'

King Lear scratched his head and said, 'I didn't know you had a pig! You had better ask your grandfather. He knows all about bath-days.' And he went on being interested in the Great Bear and the Seven Sisters in the sky. Cordelia wondered if there was a pig up there too, but she did not wait to find out.

Now Grandfather Bladud, as you know, had gone to live at the top of the Stair of the Seventy-Five Steps in the south-east corner of the fort. So Cordelia ran quickly down King Lear's fifty steps. As she passed through the courtyard her mother called out, 'Cordelia! It's your bath-day!' And the walls echoed, 'Syourbathdaydayay.' But Cordelia just kept running so that she would not forget.

When Cordelia got to the top of the Stair of the Seventy-five Steps in the south-east corner of the Great Fort, she was terribly out of breath. And when Grandfather Bladud opened the door, all he heard was the echo *bathdaydayay*. He stroked his big grey beard and wondered if it was his bath-day.

Grandmother Helen heard the echo and she said, 'Nonsense, we always have a bath on the seventh day of every month and today is the first day of *Saille*!'

Cordelia said perhaps they could go together to the pool that smells yellow, and have a happy birthday, bath-day, pig-day. Nain didn't think it was anybody's birthday and she was not interested in a pig-day, but she said, 'Would you like me to go to the nice warm pools with you and give you a swimming lesson? But,' she added, 'you will have to go and ask Great-grandfather Rud Hud Hudibras for permission. Today is not my bath-day, and he is the only person who can change it.'

So Cordelia ran all the way down the seventy-five steps of the tower in the south-east corner of the fortress, crossed the courtyard as quickly as she could, and ran up the stairs of the tower in the south-west corner.

When Cordelia reached the hundredth step of the Stair of One Hundred Steps, she stood very still and listened very carefully. She didn't want to wake her great-grandfather because then he might say no when she asked if she could go swimming with her grandmother.

Well, Great-grandfather Rud Hud Hudibras wasn't actually snoring, so Cordelia pushed the door very carefully and peeped in. There he was, looking straight at her. She could just see the space in the middle of his big white beard where he kept his mouth. Cordelia was so surprised, she blurted out as quickly as she could, 'Can I . . . please can I have a birthday for your pig?'

Great-grandfather Rud Hud Hudibras gave a great laugh that echoed round the castle walls. 'Ho-ho, ha-ha! What a splendid idea!' he roared. 'When you have had your bath, we'll have a party for all the pigs in Caer.'

Cordelia was so excited that she shrieked at the top of her voice, 'We're going to have a party! A big pig-party-party,' and the walls answered, 'Ha-ha, artypartyparty.'

Just then her mother called again, 'Bath-day, Cordelia!'

Cordelia called back, 'Artypartybath-day. Just going, Mam,' and off she went with her grandmother to the hot, bubbling pool at the bottom of the hill.

By the time they got home, all the pigs for miles around were waiting for them and making a great snuffly sort of noise in their excitement. They had a wonderful pig party and Great-grandfather said, 'Cordelia, we all have a birthday every year and a bath-day every month and I think the pigs should have a special day too! From today they will have a Grand Pig Day every year! And now would you like to choose a pig to keep for yourself?'

Cordelia chose her most favourite pig, the one that was small and pink with almost-very-nearly-magic wings. Cordelia went straight to the north-west corner of the fortress where there was no tower and began to build a very special-looking pig house.

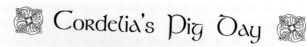

Chapter Five

In which Cordelia learns about flying

Chapter Five

One beautiful summer morning, on the harvest feast of *Lughnasadh*, the sky was blue and little puffs of wind chased the clouds. Cordelia sang a song to herself to remind her how to say *Lughnasadh*. (It sounds like Loo-nah-sah.) Then she fetched a basket and went out to find a treat for her pig.

She went down the hill, past the hot, yellow-smelling pool, and round a field where men and women were cutting and gathering the spelt to make bread. She gleaned a few stalks as she went. Then she rubbed them between her fingers to thresh out the grain. 'Pig can have grain in winter,' she murmured. 'Today, I shall find fresh melilot and buttercups.'

As she walked, she looked up at the birds overhead. She saw a golden eagle high in the sky and she wondered how it stayed up there. 'I shall ask Great-grandfather how birds fly.'

When she reached the fort on the hill, Cordelia ran to the place where there was no tower, in the north-west corner, and found her pig rooting and grunting in the mud. Her food and water dishes were kicked about all higgledy-piggledy. (Even when Cordelia asked her mother to help make Pig's pen nice and flat and tidy, Pig always dug it up again.) Pig sniffed the melilot and buttercups, and squealed with delight.

Cordelia went up the Stair of the Hundred Steps to visit Great-grandfather Rud Hud Hudibras. Sometimes Hen-daid stayed awake nearly all day and told stories about famous battles and other old stuff from long ago. Cordelia loved listening. Today, as she went up the hundred steps, she hoped he would not start a story because she knew she would forget her important question.

'Hen-daid,' she began as she opened his door. 'Can you tell me how birds fly?'

'No,' said Great-grandfather Rud Hud Hudibras, 'I am afraid I can't. I can teach you how to trap a bear but I can't tell you how birds fly. Go and ask your father.'

Cordelia walked very slowly down three steps. Then she jumped three at a time to see if she could fly. It was no good trying. She needed the secret. She ran down the other ninety-four steps, skipped across the courtyard, and climbed the fifty steps to the top of King Lear's tower.

'Dada,' she said quickly to make sure he had no time to think of something she was supposed to do. 'Can you tell me how birds fly?'

'No, I'm afraid I can't. I can tell you how the stars move in the sky but I can't tell you how birds fly. But,' he said, 'your grandmother learnt to read when she was a little girl in Greece. Perhaps she knows how birds fly. Now go and wash all that mud off your knees.'

Cordelia washed her knees in the wooden bucket that stood

near the great dining table. Then she went to look for her grandmother. Nain had just come in from the fields. She was very interested in Cordelia's question but she said, 'No, I can't tell you how birds fly but I think I know who can. Grandfather Bladud has a cloak of feathers that was given to him by the wizard, Gofannon. He may be able to tell you how birds fly.'

Cordelia was so excited by the news that she thought she would pop. She ran on ahead of her grandmother, all the way up the steps of the tower where her grandparents lived.

'Taid,' she gasped as she tried to catch her breath. 'Can you tell me how birds fly?'

'No,' said Taid, 'I can't tell you how birds fly. But I can show you my flying machine. I never really used it because the wind is so gusty round the hills of Caer. If we went down to the cliffs by the sea, perhaps it might work. Would you like to see it?'

Grandfather Bladud put on the cloak of feathers that was given to him by Gofannon, the wizard. It was supposed to help him be very wise indeed. Nain thought it was rather moth-eaten but she did not say so.

A crowd of boys and girls came out to stare when Grandfather Bladud reached the bottom of the tower. 'Would twelve boys kindly help carry my flying machine?' he asked. The boys pushed and shoved to be the chosen helpers and twelve of them ran up the stairs, two steps at a time.

They came down much more carefully, carrying the flying machine.

The twelve boys trudged all the way to the high cliffs by the sea and put down the machine facing Tara, across the water. Taid was feeling a bit stiff but he told Nain and Cordelia not to worry, and that birds found flying very relaxing.

Everybody stood on the edge of the cliff and watched. Grandfather Bladud was strapped in, and his feet were tucked up in a nice warm bag. They all waited. And then they waited some more. At last the wind was perfect. Cordelia and the boys gave a big push and Grandfather Bladud glided off the cliff. Out, out, out, over the sea he went, towards Tara, the centre of the world. Cordelia waved. Nain waved and wiped away a tiny tear. Soon he was just a speck on the horizon over the sea.

No one in Caer Badum ever saw Grandfather Bladud again.

Chapter Six

In which King Lear sees a falling star, and Cordelia meets her sisters

Cordelia always tried to visit her grandmother at least once a week in case she was lonely after Grandfather Bladud disappeared in his flying machine.

One cold morning in spring when Cordelia opened the door, Nain said, 'Cordelia, your father has been at the top of his tower for seven whole days.'

'I know,' said Cordelia, jumping from one foot to the other. 'And he stayed in his tower, thinking extra hard, all last night. Sometimes I think he is waiting for Taid to come back. This morning, the boy who carried his breakfast all the way up to the top of his tower said he wouldn't eat anything.'

'But he sent a message,' said Nain. 'He says he saw a falling star and silver rain.'

'Does he know what the silver rain means?' asked Cordelia.

'I don't know,' answered her grandmother. 'But he wants to ask Goneril and Regan to come and stay.'

Cordelia was very excited. Goneril and Regan were her sisters but they were much older and were both married. They lived so far away that she could not remember ever having seen them.

Suddenly there was a loud 'Toot! Toot!' on the nearly-magic cow horn.

'Ootoot,' went the echo. Cordelia ran as fast as she could to the Great Courtyard.

King Lear had already arrived and was looking very serious. As soon as everyone was quiet, he spoke in a great voice that seemed to shake the walls, 'Last night I saw a mighty star fall from the sky. And as it fell it shattered into a million pieces like silver rain.' Some of the people started to whisper but King Lear went on: 'The rain fell on the three great fields of Caer. It means that when I am old I must divide my kingdom into three equal parts. Each one will be called a domain and each of my daughters will rule one domain. Please send a messenger to find my daughters, Goneril and Regan, and tell them what I have decided.'

There were gasps. There were groans. There was whispering and there was wailing. Nearly everyone had forgotten about the twin princesses, Goneril and Regan.

'They never even visit Caer,' said someone. 'They have kingdoms of their own,' said another. 'They are married to strangers from foreign lands,' said a third. Cordelia couldn't wait to see them.

After about a year there was still no news and everyone began to forget about the twin princesses. Pig had grown big and strong. Most days, if the sun was shining, Cordelia would put on her rabbit-fur hat and race Pig around the whole fort. Then one day when they had run all the way round the inside, they decided to run right round the outside.

They went through the opening in the first rampart, past the guard, who said, 'Nice day!'

Then Pig and Cordelia raced down the narrow passage and out through the second rampart. The slope on either side was thick with young oak trees and brambles. Pig sniffed. Suddenly she was off. Although she sometimes stopped and raised her snout to sniff again, Cordelia could hardly keep up. She slipped and slithered and fell on her knees. She caught her tunic on a bramble and made a hole. 'Stop, Pig!' she shouted, but Pig took no notice and kept on running.

When Pig reached the bottom of the woody slope, she turned round and sniffed some more. Cordelia ran to catch hold of her. But Pig had found what she really wanted. Truffles. She dug furiously, first with her hooves then with her snout, grunting all the while. There were enough truffles to satisfy even the greediest pig and Cordelia collected as many as she could carry to save for another day.

It was difficult climbing the slope again so Cordelia and Pig followed a little badger path until they came to the track that led up to the main entrance. Just as they reached it, Cordelia heard a noise like an army approaching.

At first she was very frightened. 'What could that be?' she said aloud. Then she began to wonder if it just might be her sisters arriving. She crept forward with Pig and peered over a bush. They could see a crowd moving towards them but still quite a long way off. Cordelia was sure it must be Goneril and Regan. She looked at her torn tunic and her dirty knees.

'Oh, Pig!' she exclaimed. 'What will Mam say? We had better go and wash before my sisters arrive!'

Cordelia didn't have much puff left and Pig didn't really want to wash but they trotted along together towards the yellow-smelling pool where Cordelia usually had her bath. Pig had a quick splash and ran towards the track again to watch. Cordelia began to wash carefully, first her hands and then her face. She was just going to start on her knees when there was a terrible squealing.

'Poor Pig!' she shouted. 'What's the matter?' Pig didn't hear her. No one heard her. And Cordelia was only just in time to see a man picking up Pig and putting her in the back of a chariot.

There were two shiny chariots and hundreds of servants following on foot. The first chariot was drawn by two proud-looking horses and a woman was whipping them to make them go faster. In the second stood a woman in a golden headdress that looked more like a helmet than a crown. Cordelia decided she had to help Pig and she ran after them as fast as she could.

Cordelia could not get near the first chariot because the wheels were as sharp as knives but she called out in her loudest voice, 'Excuse me! Excuse me! Could you please stop. I think you have my pig in your chariot!'

Goneril couldn't remember anyone ever daring to shout at her and she said, 'Her pig, indeed! Who is this dirty child, stopping my chariot and shouting?'

'Hush!' said Regan. 'I think she might be our sister.'

Cordelia didn't know what to feel. She didn't think the rude lady would be a very nice sister.

'Child,' continued Regan, 'are you Cordelia?' Cordelia nodded and Regan told a man to pick her up and put her in the chariot. Cordelia didn't want to be put in the chariot and she certainly didn't want to be picked up. She tried to explain about Pig, but Regan said, 'Oh, dear no! That pig will make a very nice supper! Now jump in and sit down and we'll drive to the fort.'

When Regan's chariot reached the first gate to the fort, Cordelia could hear a great commotion. Goneril's chariot had passed through the gate in the first rampart but was too wide to go through the gate in the second rampart. It was stuck. The passage between the two gates was too narrow to turn round and the horses refused to go backwards.

King Lear was looking very worried and Goneril was looking furious. Cordelia's mother was saying, 'There, there!' to the horses and trying to look cheerful.

At that moment, Pig wriggled free and jumped out of the chariot, narrowly missing the horses' hooves. The horses were so alarmed at seeing a pink pig rushing between them and waving her curly tail, that they backed quickly down the narrow passage. In no time at all, they were out of the first gate and would have galloped all the way home if Regan's chariot hadn't been blocking their path. The two chariots crashed together and the noise rang out for miles around.

Goneril climbed down from the chariot but Regan was so shaken up that she had to be helped.

'There, there!' said King Lear, holding out his arms to his two daughters.

'There, there,' said Cordelia, leaning forward to Goneril's horses. 'It was only a pig.'

'Only a pig!' screamed Goneril. 'We might have all been killed!'

But no one was hurt and the twin princesses soon felt much better.

'Welcome home,' said Queen Rheinid as she kissed her daughters. And they all went to the Grand Courtyard where men were roasting five huge oxen and preparing a great feast.

Chapter Seven

In which Cordelia makes a promise

The following morning, the world had turned white. Snow had been falling all night and the trees sparkled with frost and snow. Pig wanted to go out for a run immediately but Cordelia told her to wait. She was afraid Pig might get caught again. But Goneril and Regan were nowhere to be seen. They slept all morning and even a little bit into the afternoon.

When they finally appeared, Goneril said, 'I hope someone has locked up that wild pig!'

Cordelia pretended not to hear.

Regan said, 'I shall get my feet wet in all this snow. I would like to be carried.'

Cordelia ran to fetch her best new boots so that her sister would not get wet feet. But when she returned with a boot in each hand, Regan had been carried to a seat near the big fire and was busy warming her toes.

King Lear came and sat down too. He was very pleased to see his three daughters all together. 'Now,' he said, 'I want to explain why I have sent for you.' And he told them all about the falling star and the silver rain that fell on the three great fields of Caer.

'It is a sign,' he said. 'I shall divide my kingdom into three parts. Each one will be called a domain and, when I get old, each of you will rule one domain.'

'Which is my domain?' asked Goneril and, before King Lear could answer, Regan said, 'I want the domain with the magic water.'

Cordelia thought they were very rude but she did not say a word.

King Lear was a bit upset when he heard them. He wanted to change his mind but he knew that kings have to keep their word. Then he had a good idea. 'I will decide which one can choose first when I find out who loves me most.'

Goneril thought this was a silly idea but she said, 'I do!' in a voice that sounded like freezing rain.

Regan thought it was a silly idea too, but she cried out as loudly as she could, 'I love you more than anyone in the world!' in a voice that sounded like rusty wheels.

Cordelia didn't know what to say and she kept very quiet indeed. She thought it would be quite nice to be given a domain but she thought it would be more fun to have a husband and lots of children. 'Maybe they could all keep pigs,' she thought.

King Lear looked at her. He had a big smile and he was waiting for her to say something.

'I love you, Father,' she said very quietly.

'How much?' teased King Lear and he laughed a great big laugh.

'Well,' said Cordelia slowly, 'a bit more than Pig . . .' and she wanted to say, 'just exactly the same as Mam.'

But Goneril and Regan started to snigger.

King Lear stopped laughing. He even stopped smiling and began to frown.

'. . . But I think when I have a husband I will love him a bit more.'

Goneril and Regan exploded with laughter. 'She'll only get a very small domain,' whispered Regan.

'I wouldn't give her a domain at all,' muttered Goneril.

King Lear said, 'When I am an old man and you are grown-up, I hope you will give me a better answer.' And he walked off in a huff.

Queen Rheinid put her arm round Cordelia and squeezed her hand.

Then Goneril and Regan went out and started to draw lines in the snow. They didn't ask Cordelia to come with them. She heard a lot of stamping and arguing.

'I want that hill,' shrieked Regan.

'You've already claimed the magic pool!' yelled Goneril.

Cordelia went off to find Pig.

That evening Goneril and Regan went home without saying goodbye, and even King Lear was quite glad when they had gone.

Cordelia picked up all the clothes they had left lying around and tried them on. They were much too big and she couldn't imagine being grown-up and wearing such grand robes. Her mother laughed a lot when she saw her and King Lear looked a bit less grumpy.

Cordelia really wanted to make her father smile. First she promised she wouldn't ask any more questions for at least three days. But he went on looking grumpy and sad.

Then she tried: 'I'll be extra good and keep my knees clean for at least five days.' But he didn't smile.

Finally she sat down very close beside him and whispered in his ear, 'Dada, I'll love you for ever and ever!' King Lear smiled a very small smile and he took Cordelia in his arms and hugged her. But when he let her go, she saw he had tears in his eyes.

'Do you remember I told you about the falling star and the silver rain?' he said.

Cordelia nodded.

'I don't know if I really understand it all yet,' he went on. Cordelia sat very still because she could see that he was thinking. Then he said, 'You are a very clever girl. Would you like to study the heavens with me?'

Cordelia jumped up. She couldn't think of anything more

wonderful and she wanted to shout at the top of her voice. But then she thought for a moment and said, 'Would I still have time to visit Nain and . . . and . . . what about Pig? Could I still take her for a walk every day?'

At last King Lear laughed. His youngest daughter really was very clever and very kind. He knew she would be a very good astronomer and he hoped that one day, when the time came, she would help him to divide his kingdom. 'I think you should visit Nain as often as you want to and you'll certainly have to look after Pig,' he said. 'Then, when you are ready, you can climb the stairs to the top of my tower and I'll teach you everything I know.'

'Everything you know!' cried Cordelia, clapping her hands.

And the listening walls answered: 'Knowowowo!'

Glossary and Notes

Bronze (page 13)
Bronze is made from copper with tin added. Copper probably came from Pen y Gogarth near Llanduno and tin from Cornwall. The Bronze Age is the period when bronze was used to make weapons, armour, knives and ornaments. By 700 BC people in Britain had also learned how to use iron, so we call this the Iron Age. Cordelia lived in the Iron Age.

Brush and comb (page 10)
No one has found an Iron Age brush yet but we know the people were very clever with tools and would probably have made brushes for their own hair and for their animals. Bone combs from Cordelia's time, and possibly much earlier, have been dug up. You can see one at Castell Henllys in the Pembrokeshire Coast National Park.

Celtic months (page 35)
Cordelia practises saying the names of the Celtic months: *Beth, Luis, Nion, Fearn* and *Saille*. As each month starts when the moon is full, there are thirteen months in a year and each month has twenty-eight days. The other months are called *Huath, Duir, Tinne, Coll, Muir, Gort, Ngetal* and *Ruis*. They are all named after trees and other plants.

Elm (page 22)
You may never have seen an elm because these trees, which used to grow all over Britain, were attacked by a fungus called Dutch Elm Disease. It had killed most elms by about 1970. Nowadays, elm trees in the wild usually start to die as soon as they get to about four metres tall.

Flint (page 9)
Flint is a very hard stone which can be split to make sharp tools. This is called knapping. Cordelia's family would almost certainly also have used sharp knives made of iron.

Hill Forts (page 5)

Hill forts were built by the people of Britain before the Romans arrived and you can find them all over Wales. (The better-known ones are often marked on maps but you may be able to discover one that hardly anyone visits.) They are often on the tops of hills, quite high up and must have been used to defend a number of families and their animals against raiders. Others, like Caer, are built on lower hills but still have a good view all the way round. Some sites, such as Castell Dinas near Crickhowell in Powys, and Llansteffan Castle near Carmarthen, were redesigned and reused in the Middle Ages because the Iron Age people had found such good positions.

Melilot (page 43)

Melilot is a meadow plant rather like clover. It has a small yellow flower and each leaf is divided into three leaflets.

Spelt (page 26)

Spelt is a kind of wheat that was grown in Iron Age Britain. People have started to cultivate it again as they believe it is particularly healthy and, if you are lucky, you may be able to find a loaf of spelt bread in your local bakery.

Yellow-smelling water (page 13)

Water like this still flows in Bath today and has iron, magnesium, copper, potassium, and radium in it. People go and bathe there because they believe it is very healthy. The temperature of the water bubbling out of the earth is about 46°C. A swimming pool is usually about 29°C, so Cordelia would have found it quite nice to take a dip even in March!

Published in Wales in 2011 by Pont Books, an imprint of
Gomer Press, Llandysul, Ceredigion, SA44 4JL

ISBN 978 1 84851 233 7

A CIP record for this title is available from the British Library.

© Copyright text: Elizabeth Byrne Hill, 2011
© Copyright illustrations: Kate Aldous, 2011

Elizabeth Byrne Hill and Kate Aldous assert their moral right
under the Copyright, Designs and Patents Act, 1988
to be identified respectively as author and illustrator of this work.

This book is published with the financial support of the Welsh Books Council.

Printed and bound in Wales at Gomer Press, Llandysul, Ceredigion